DUCKWORTH

the Difficult Child

To difficult children everywhere

—M.S.

For Carmela, with all my love

—J.S.

ATHENEUM BOOKS FOR YOUNG READERS
An imprint of Simon & Schuster Children's Publishing Division
1230 Avenue of the Americas, New York, New York 10020
Text copyright © 2019 by Michael Sussman
Illustrations copyright © 2019 by Júlia Sardà
ATHENEUM BOOKS FOR YOUNG READERS is a registered trademark of Simon & Schuster, Inc.
Atheneum logo is a trademark of Simon & Schuster, Inc.
For information about special discounts for bulk purchases, please contact Simon & Schuster Special Sales at
1-866-506-1949 or business@simonandschuster.com.
The Simon & Schuster Speakers Bureau can bring authors to your live event. For more information or to book an event,
contact the Simon & Schuster Speakers Bureau at 1-866-248-3049 or visit our website at www.simonspeakers.com.
Book design by Sonia Chaghatzbanian
The text for this book was set in ITC Cheltenham Std.
The illustrations for this book were rendered digitally.
Manufactured in China
0419 SCP
First Edition
2 4 6 8 10 9 7 5 3 1
Library of Congress Cataloging-in-Publication Data
Names: Sussman, Michael, author. I Sardà, Júlia, illustrator.
Title: Duckworth, the difficult child / Michael Sussman ; Illustrated by Júlia Sardà.
Description: First edition. I New York : Atheneum Books for Young Readers, [2019] I Summary: When Duckworth finds a
snake in his closet, and then is swallowed whole, his parents are sure he is simply being difficult.
Identifiers: LCCN 2017041514 I ISBN 9781534405127 (hardcover) I ISBN 9781534405134 (eBook)
Subjects: I CYAC: Parent and child—Fiction. I Snakes—Fiction. I Humorous stories.
Classification: LCC PZ7.S96568 Duc 2019 I DDC [E]—dc23
LC record available at https://lccn.loc.gov/2017041514

DUCKWORTH

the Difficult Child

Written by Michael Sussman
Illustrated by Júlia Sardà

 Atheneum Books for Young Readers · New York   London   Toronto   Sydney   New Delhi

D uckworth was building a castle out of toothpicks when he heard a hissing sound.

He looked up and saw a gigantic snake slithering out of his closet.

Duckworth dashed downstairs, where he found his parents sitting together on the sofa. They were reading a book called *Dealing with Your Difficult Child.*

"A huge snake came out of my closet," said Duckworth. "I think it's a cobra."

"According to this book," said Mother, "you are too old to be imagining monsters under the bed, Duckworth. Or snakes hiding in your closet, for that matter."

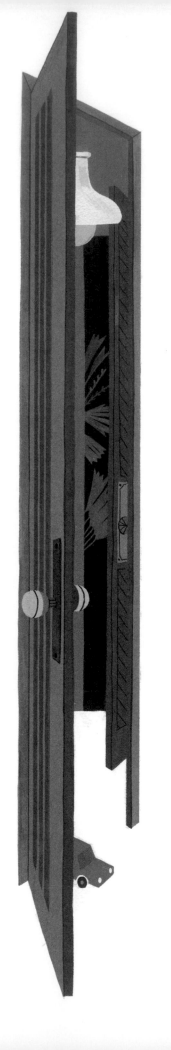

"But it's a *real* snake," Duckworth insisted. "It hissed at me."

"It's all in your head," said Father. "It says here you will forget such nonsense if we give you chores to do. Please wash the dishes, Duckworth, and when you're done with that, take out the garbage and mow the lawn."

By the time Duckworth finished his chores, he was so tired that he had, in fact, forgotten all about the snake.

But after taking a nap, Duckworth was practicing his recorder when the cobra slithered right up and . . .

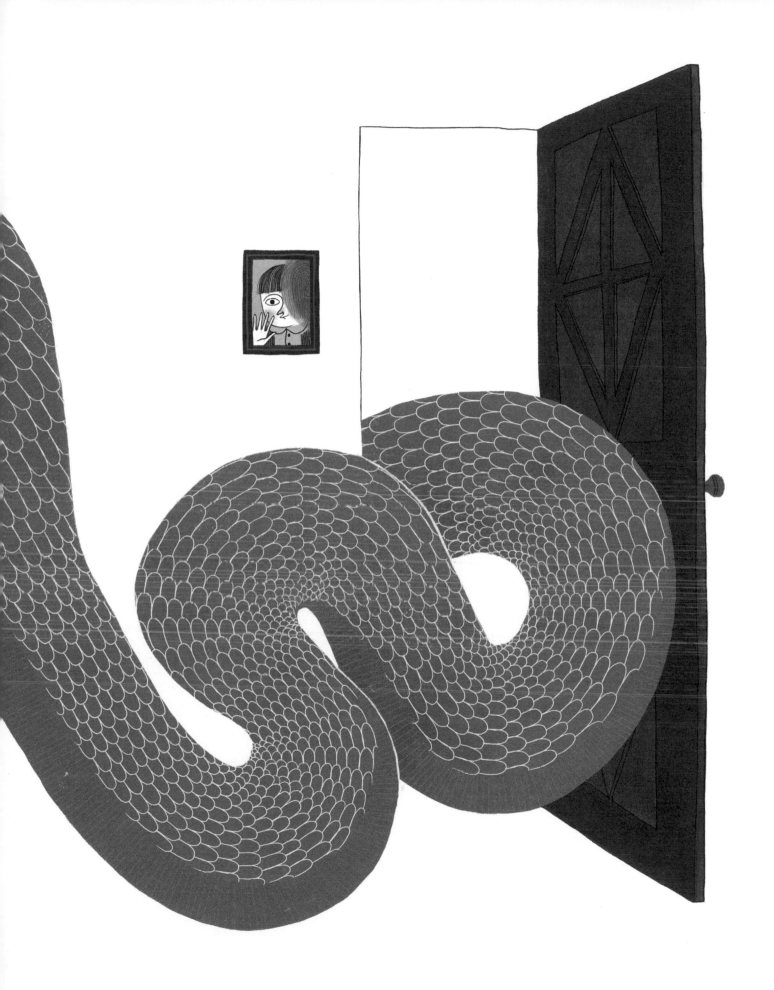

swallowed him whole!

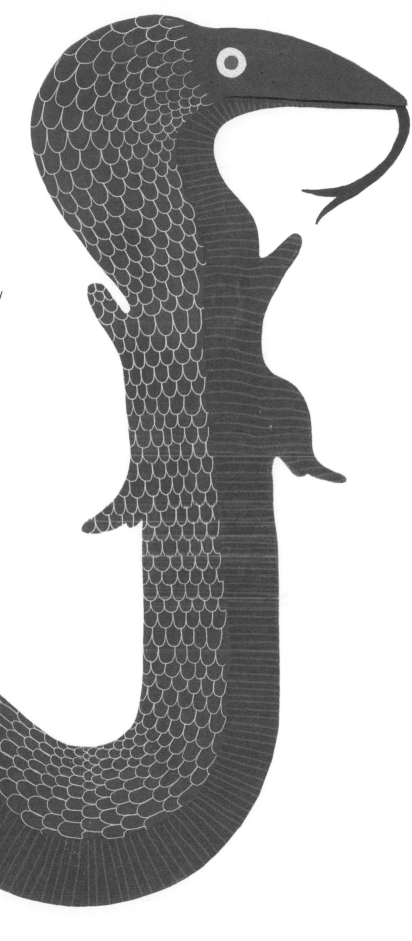

The snake slid downstairs and into the game room, where Duckworth's parents were playing checkers.

"Where did you find that snake costume?" asked Father.

"It's not a costume," said Duckworth from inside the cobra. "The snake from my closet swallowed me."

"It's crazy ideas like these that make you such a difficult child," said Mother. "The book says your fantasies will go away if we ignore them."

So while Father prepared dinner, Mother continued
playing checkers.

Somehow, the snake managed to win.

Father called everyone to the table. The snake slithered up onto Duckworth's chair.

"The book says we're supposed to include Duckworth in mealtime conversations," said Mother.

"Excellent," said Father. "How was your day, Duckworth?"

"Terrible," said Duckworth. "I'm stuck inside a snake."

"Please use your knife and fork, Duckworth," said Mother. "You're too old to be eating like an animal."

After dinner, Duckworth's parents went out for a stroll. The snake followed them.

They met Mr. and Mrs. Snodgrass and stopped to chat.

"I see Duckworth's wearing his snake costume," said Mr. Snodgrass.

"It's not a costume!" cried Duckworth. "A snake swallowed me!"

"Oh my!" Mrs. Snodgrass said with a chuckle. "What a vivid imagination!"

"Yes," Mother agreed. "That's what makes him such a difficult child."

"Luckily, we bought a book on how to handle difficult children like Duckworth," said Father. "It says to keep him busy with playmates. So tonight we've invited his cousin Digby for a sleepover."

"Oh no!" cried Duckworth. "The snake will swallow Digby too!"

"Don't be ridiculous," Mother laughed. "Digby is afraid of the dark. He'd never get inside your silly costume."

Digby won't have any choice, thought Duckworth. He had to free himself at once.

Fortunately, by the time they got home, Duckworth had thought of a plan.

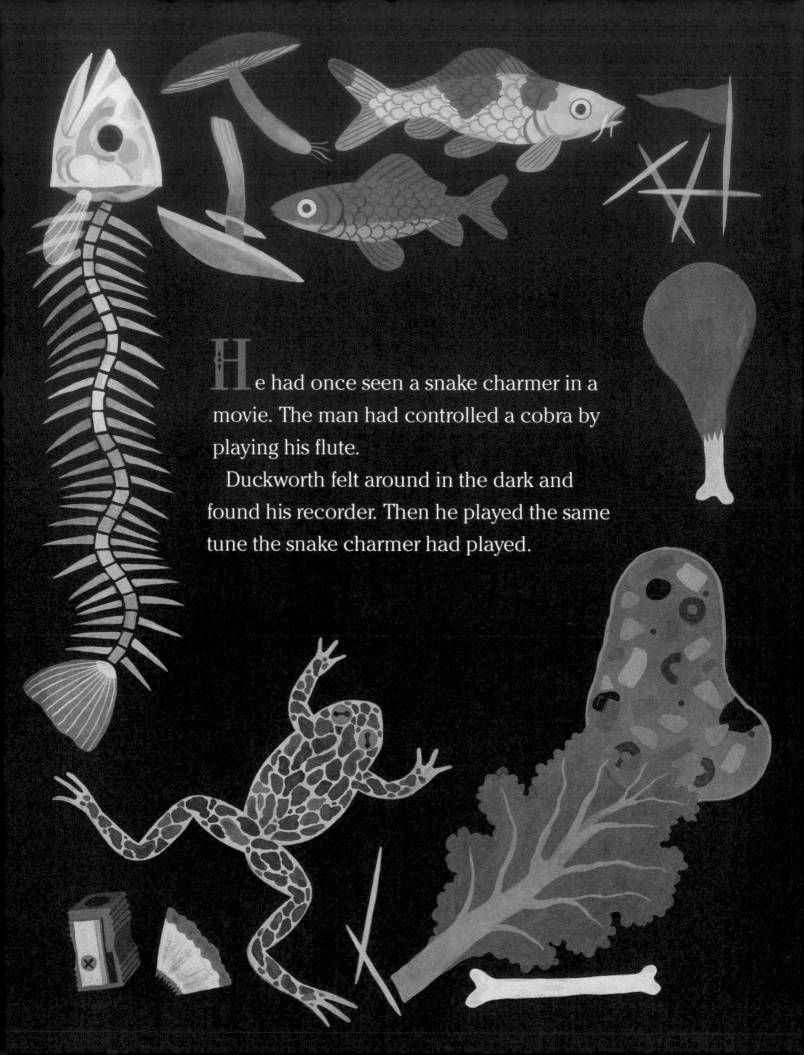

He had once seen a snake charmer in a movie. The man had controlled a cobra by playing his flute.

Duckworth felt around in the dark and found his recorder. Then he played the same tune the snake charmer had played.

Sure enough, the snake opened its
mouth wide . . .
and Duckworth crawled out.

"It's about time you took off that silly costume," said Father.

"Now please put it back in your closet until Halloween," said Mother.

Duckworth let the snake out the back door.

As he watched it slither away into the bushes, he wondered where he could find a book for dealing with difficult parents.